For Maisie

A Red Fox Book
Published by Random House Children's Books
20 Vauxhall Bridge Road, London SW1V 2SA
A division of The Random House Group Ltd
London Melbourne Sydney Auckland
Johannesburg and agencies throughout the world

Copyright text and illustrations © Ron Maris 1994

1 3 5 7 9 10 8 6 4 2

First published in Great Britain by Julia MacRae 1994
Red Fox edition 1999

Printed in Singapore

RANDOM HOUSE UK Limited Reg. No. 954009

ISBN 0 09 187309 6

LITTLE
GINGER

Ron Maris

RED FOX

Little Ginger had no home.

"Buzz off!" said Mr Carpenter.
"Grr..!" growled Mr Carpenter's dog.

"Shoo!" shouted Mrs Potter.
"Shoo!" shouted Mrs Potter's parrot.

"Go away!" said Mr Gardener.
"Baa!" bleated Mr Gardener's goat.

"Hello, Little Ginger," said Mrs Farmer.

"Talk to Cow and Sheep and Hen and
see if they will let you stay."

"Please can I stay?"
said Little Ginger to Cow.
"What do you do?" said Cow.

"Nothing much," said Little Ginger.
"What do *you* do?"

"I used to give milk," said Cow,
"but not any more."

"Please can I stay?"
said Little Ginger to Sheep.
"What do you do?" said Sheep.

"Nothing much," said Little Ginger.
"What do *you* do?"

"I used to give wool," said Sheep,
"but not any more."

"Please can I stay?"
said Little Ginger to Hen.
"What do you do?" said Hen.

"Nothing much," said Little Ginger.
"What do *you* do?"

"I used to lay eggs," said Hen,
"but not any more."

"What's wrong with you all?"
said Little Ginger.

"RATS!" said Cow and Sheep and Hen.
"There are so many of them. They take
all our food and they give us no peace.
We can't eat and we can't sleep."

"Well," said Little Ginger.

"I'll just walk around a bit . . .

and sit in the sun a bit . . .

and let the rats see that I'm here.
That is what *I* do."

And away ran the rats into the woods,
as fast and as far as they could go,
leaving the farmyard in peace.

So Cow gave milk again,

... and Sheep gave wool again,

... and Hen laid eggs again.

"Do stay for ever,"
said Cow and Sheep and Hen.

And Little Ginger did.

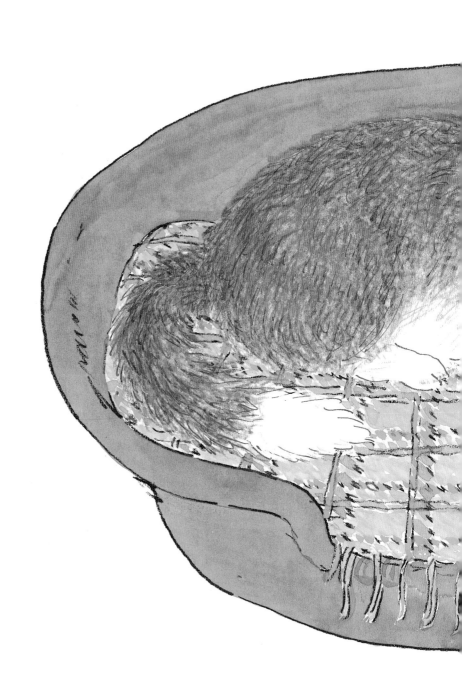

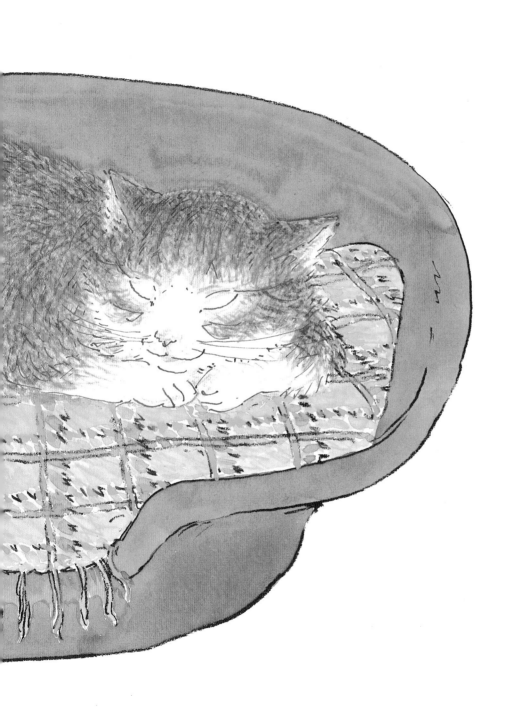

Some bestselling Red Fox picture books

THE BIG ALFIE AND ANNIE ROSE STORYBOOK
by Shirley Hughes
OLD BEAR
by Jane Hissey
OI! GET OFF OUR TRAIN
by John Burningham
DON'T DO THAT!
by Tony Ross
NOT NOW, BERNARD
by David McKee
ALL JOIN IN
by Quentin Blake
THE WHALES' SONG
by Gary Blythe and Dyan Sheldon
JESUS' CHRISTMAS PARTY
by Nicholas Allan
THE PATCHWORK CAT
by Nicola Bayley and William Mayne
WILLY AND HUGH
by Anthony Browne
THE WINTER HEDGEHOG
by Ann and Reg Cartwright
A DARK, DARK TALE
by Ruth Brown
HARRY, THE DIRTY DOG
by Gene Zion and Margaret Bloy Graham
DR XARGLE'S BOOK OF EARTHLETS
by Jeanne Willis and Tony Ross
WHERE'S THE BABY
by Pat Hutchins